SHANE VAN ROOYEN

The Missing Piece, The Hole in my Heart.

English(the hole in my heart) true life sory

Contents

Preface

Introduction

The missing piece, the hole in my heart, written by Shane Marquin van Rooyen, it is a book written by myself based on the true life events I faced in life, the people, their names and the names of the places mentioned in the book is all real.

The book was written in my own words, in a very simple and understandable way , so that every reader can understand the book, it contains information about the experiences, events and happenings I have had as a child from the age of 6 years old up to an adult of 27 years old. In this book the reader will be inform how I was once a normal child, who also had big dreams for the future ahead of me, but I somehow got lost along the way on my path that I was traveling on. In the manuscript the reader will be inform, how I got lost and how I was able to find my way back in later years of my life, what sacrifices it took for me to be found again. The book is based on my past life, but it also brings the reality of the present we are currently living in, and it brings to us the assurance of the hope that there is for everyone a future in life who longs for it. It also serves as a special treatment for the spiritual, physical and menthol health of the human being as a reader. The stories and events in this book once again are all true, and it will show the reader how easy we can be damage without even recognized it. It will show you how I experienced,realized,recognized and accepted, the missing piece in my heart. This book material also serves as a tool to encourage someone out there in the world, that no matter what you are facing in life , there is always a way out. This book is written to all ages, you may be a youngster or an adult, a child, a mom or a dad, but in this book is a little something for everyone. The book contains information of hope and will-power, for everyone and it is the idea to share my knowledge, my love, my understanding in life and my experiences to every reader by putting it on paper and pen, to tell you that all things are possible by God, as soon as we recognize and accept that we do or may have a weakness or a problem in life.

Sometimes we do not know what to do, or where to go with what we are facing , but if we take the step in faith to search for the better and we accept that we do have a problem, life will turn His face towards us and eventually it will get better , because life was and is given unto us as a gift from God, and we have to find our way in life back to enjoy the gift of life, if we somehow went lost.

This book was inspired by the grace of God upon my life and the inspiration and the power of the Holy spirit, His love and His mercy.

God speaks to us on a daily basis, from the day we were born, to the day we die.

We do not always recognize the voice of God in our daily lives at all, but as time goes by we come to our awareness that it was God who was speaking.

He speaks in love, by His word and all His grace that is always available for us and he goes before us by his spirit, although we don't recognize it instantly. In this book you will read of many different events that took place in my life, up till I meet with God in person, and the way He connected with me through his grace and His Love.

The book serves also as an education lesson to those who want to learn from it, wich we all can somehow learn. It is a book of faith, the normal life in general as a human being, and a spiritual book that can encourage someone to never give up, but we have to push through, because there is a greater and higher power who is always looking over us and looking out for us.

This book contains powerful events and how God molded me, from a child to an adult.

In this book you will also read about my first one on one encounter with God and his angels, and how He took care of me when I couldn't took care of myself, with His angels on several times and events in my life

I hope that this book will encourage and inspire someone, gives someone new hope, and a new outlook on the world we are in and wich surrounds us.

This is a book of uplifting, a book that brings back hope, where it seems to be no more hope, and a book based on faith.

Without faith, it is impossible to reach out to God.

It is the prayer of my heart that through the grace of God and the information in this book, that people shall be restore and become whole again.

And like the promise of God still stand, that He is near to those who are broken hearted.

In this book you ,the reader will experience true testimonies, a once broken heart, a damage heart with an empty space, searching to be fixed again, and the importance of it all, the search, the recognizen, the acceptance and the fixing, wich is the healing.

Word of encouragement:
    Matthew 12:20
    A bruised reed he will not break,
    and a smoldering wick he will not snuff out,
    till he has brought justice through to victory.

In other words:
    He won't brush aside the bruised and broken. He will be gentle
with the weak and feeble, until his victory releases justice.

Shane van Rooyen.

Chapter 1

The Unknown:

I was born on 24 April 1979, I was raised by a single parent, a woman which I called "mommy". Her name was Rosie van Rooyen. (Dolla was her nickname)She was one of three daughters and four brothers.

Up till today, I am still calling her 'mommy'.

I was the only child of my mother back then,for the first 6 years of my life, then suddenly something new happened in our files, my mother got pregnant and gave birth to another baby boy, he was called my brother, named Randall.

At the time I was only 6 years old and for me it was the most exited news ever heard, definitely it was something new in my life but what an exited experience it was, because now I was not alone as a child in the house anymore, but I had a new friend that I could call my brother and play with.

I always thought that I was going to be the only child of my mother, but then this really good thing happened to us, a new member was added to our family , it was an awesome feeling, and I was very exited about it, because, although he was just a small little baby boy, he attracted our attention very much.

We, grew up together as brothers in peace and love for the

following 3 years my life , from 6 years old till I became 9 years of age. We stayed on a farm, called "Levin se plaas" as we knew it back then, the original name of the farm was "Champaighn Farms", it was a farm also located in Wellington Western Cape South Africa on Piet Retief and Champaighn Road, surrounded with the most beautiful mountains around Wellington. Today, there is a retire resort complex, on the ground where the farm used to be.

I was not very used to a big group of people at all and the only people I used to know on my age at the time, was my mother, my little brother, an aunt of mine who was my mother's younger sister, my grandmother and grandfather, because we shared the same house and we called it home.

Sometimes, I saw another woman came by from somewhere else in town and then she would visited us and as the time went by I've heard in an explanation to me that she was the other sister of my mother and that she was the eldest. Her name was Rachel.Then I met her children, she had three children, a older son Jacquin, and two daughters Loretta and Rochelle. Now I knew that they were also family of mine.

So from time to time they would came and visited us at our farm house where we stayed. We as children, cousins and nephews loved each other so much, we would play together without any fighting and shouting or creaming on each other, we just loved to do our own things. The bound of love between us as a family were strong enough to keep us going forward in unity, for me it felt like nothing would ever come and destroy a love so strong connected like our bound.

Then my aunt, Rachel also got pregnant and she gave birth to another son, wich became the youngest of her children and his name was Ruaan-Patrick. We also had a nickname for him and we called him Poena. He died on a very young age.

Now, she had four children.

Ruaan and my brother Randall, they were around the same age, a couple of months differents between them I think and we as children really loved and enjoyed each others companies very dearly.

So I was part of a beautiful and smart family, wich I never new before, Me and my brother grew up under the provision and the protection of a mom, she was indeed our everything.

In the mornings, I saw her standing up, got herself ready and dressed up, she would make sure that I was also dressed up for school, a bag would be packed for my little brother with everything he would need for the day and then she would say, "Moenie stout wees nie hoor, mammie gaan werk toe". Then she would take her stuff and leave home.

So every morning she went out for work, to take care of me and my little brother.

I didn't know what it was all about, but I trusted her, and my brother was at that time not mature enough in age ,to understand a thing. When she went to her day task, wich was a hairdresser at a well-known hair salon in town, we had to stay by our grandparents.

Our grandparents were "auntie Rosie" and "oom Gert van Rooyen."

They were looking after us, while my mom was at work. They were the most and very kind people I ever knew and I really loved and trusted them so much. When it was pension-pay day, they usually took us as grandchildren out on the trip with them to pension-pay and treated us for the day.

So we were raised by a single mom and the support of our

grandparents. In our beautiful picture of life was no biological dad or dads at all. Me and my brother were step, we didn't have the same biological father, but we were definitely from the same mother, raised in unity in love.

We didn't know about a dad, or a father figure at all, and the weirdest feeling at all was that we never knew that a dad was something that really exist.

My eldest aunt was married, they stayed in the other side of town called Payton place (Hillcrest).One day, her children invited me to come and sleep over for a night at their house, I asked my mother if I could go and she said, "yes, you may go and stay the night."

All of a sudden, while I was at their house, a new unknown person entered my space in the house and I was blown away, because never ever in my life, had I saw this man before and he was speaking to my family with a loud and hard voice, the only question that went through my mind was, "what is happening here?"

Then I got told by my cousins that it was their dad.

" A dad, What is a dad?" went through my little small mind, and they explained to me.

So they had a dad, me and my brother we didn't have any of it at all and I could not understand anything about it, I started to question my mother about the dad situation.

My mother couldn't gave me the straight explanation or answer, all she always said to me was, "You don't have a dad."

So that started to hurt me inside, on the age of 6 years old, I found out, that a dad, a father does not exist in my life or my brothers' lives at all.

I also went to school, on the age of 6 years old,my first year at a school called Hillcrest Primary school in Wellington, it was the the year of 1986. So everyday I walked from the school to home.

One thing I was never familiar to was "fear," I didn't knew that something called fear even exist.

And on the age of 6 years old, I had my first encounter with fear and how it felt to become afraid of something you didn't asked for and I experienced what fear actually can do to someone.

One day while I was coming from school, I was walking along all by myself, although many other children also walked towards their houses, a boy very older than me came out of the blue, dressed in his white school shirt and grey trousers. Angry he ran towards me and he punched me with his fist on my mouth and then again on my nose. I started to bled from my nose.

I was shocked, because I did not know this boy at all, or where he came from, but he had hit me.

To be true to you, I was just a normal boy, I didn't no anything about violence or fights or arguing at all , because I never saw things like that happened to me in my life and all of a sudden I became a victim of something I was not familiar to.

From that day I felt so afraid and my walks to school and out of school was not the same anymore, because I had to be on the look out for someone that might be run up to me and hurt me again.

And fear entered my life.

My second year of school I attended another school called Pauw Gedenk Primary school for two years in 1987–1988.

And that two years was from the best years and experiences of my childhood life.

I was introduced to many other souls, human beings that I

didn't know before, never did I know that people like them exist, but I was overwhelmed by their presents in my life. One of my friends was Le-Roy Kroneberg. He became my best friend at the time. I really liked him and how he treated me. We were friends up till the end of our primary school years. Every day after school, me and him would come together and play together. We used to play at his house in Kroneberg street right behind the Library, where we used to go. He also played the piano and he was in music school. He also told me about some stuff on the piano and I could learn small things with big matters from him. We were just kids and till today I remember the lessons I could learn from him. Today me and Le- Roy are not that close anymore, because our life paths went into different directions on an early age, but we are still friends that I can be sure of. Today, He is a professional pianist and keyboard player and his name is on the list and highlights amongst many others. I definitely learned a lot from him, the one thing I can be sure of is that dreams can come true, because when we were just boys playing around with our toys and doing our homework as kids, his dream was always to become a professional pianist one day and he did it. He chased his dream.

So yes, we must never give up on our dreams or our children's dreams no matter how life is treating us, but keep on pressing towards the goals in our lives.

And so I became friends with many other boys and girls at Pauw Gedenk Primary school, friends I never had before and my circle of knowing other people was now getting bigger.

They all became part of my life journey.

And I experienced love in many different ways, because of the love I received from home, but also the love I received from the teachers and learners who were connected to my life during

1986-1988. I remember this one woman, who used to work at school in the kitchen ,she always prepared soup for the kids at school and she always said to me," You are my child, come sit here". Her name was also auntie Rachel, she was a very dear and kind person.

For that 3 years of my educational years 1986-1989, I became one of the top learners at Pauw Gedenk Primary school, I even end up in news papers as one of top learners, three years in a row.

It was always between me and Le-roy, I also remember Inge, sometimes another name also came through, but it was highlighted times for all of us.

I took place in the school's drama classes and events, I attended the school choir.

My mom was so proud of me, but deep down inside of me was the unknown, busy to damage a beautiful soul. The unknown in my life started with the consciousness on my mind and the feeling in my heart of the absents of a father figure, a dad that was not a part of me at all. And all of a sudden fear entered my life, because I didn't feel safe anymore and the lack of protection of a father that was absent was starting to eat me from the inside. At first I did not realized it, but it was there, starting to grow from a bad seed that was planted in fertile soil.

The Unknown became a part of a destruction in my heart and on mind.

The school usually held parent nights, and moms and dads would came out to have a look at their children's achievements and books, and I saw that my new friends they all have dads, but I don't have anyone like a dad and that has hurt me so much more.

Hurt was created by a father figure who never showed up in

my life, when I needed him.

It became so sad inside of me and the smile I used to have on my face as a child started to fade slowly but surely away.

My mother took the courage and she put me to baptized and sent me to Sunday school, at the N.G Sending Church in Wellington, where she also was a member.

There, I met many of my school friends and classmates and we could catch up.

I enjoyed every moment of Sunday school. I didn't know that all this stuff that I was learning from at Sunday school is the foundation in my life, that God was laying down for me , and someday I might need it again on my life journey ahead.

And my mother made sure that a strong foundation was laid upon me.

On the age of six I had several encounters with God, things that happened in my life, but for me, I didn't understand it at all, I had visions, I had dreams, I had moments where I just felt that I don't fit into this specific world, but I didn't understand it at all.

Some of my dreams were about things that seemed so real, like if it was a reality and when time passes by I would remember this was actually what I dreamed about. I did see a lot of numbers in my dreams, I had time traveling dreams, but I did not understand any of it at all.

Today, I realize it was God all the time, I realize that I am special, but I didn't know it back then.

And that is how God made everyone of us on this earth.

We are all gifted, talented and special , in an unique way so that He can be glorified, we are all called for a purpose and something greater, but somehow we all get lost on the roads we are traveling and we had to find our way back.

Whatever we go through in life is just experiences and we have to learn from it.

We were born to become living testimonies for the saving of another person's life.

And that's why we get lost sometimes we get blindfolded by the the lies of the enemy wich is our prosecutor in this world, and it give us opportunities, decisions and choices to choose from. Our decisions decides wich way we are headed to.

Word of encouragement:

Isaiah 42:16

And I will bring the blind by a way that they knew not; I will lead them in paths that they have not known: I will make darkness light before them, and crooked things straight. These things will I do unto them, and not forsake them.

Chapter 2

The Searhing:

I became nine years old, three years from the age of six has passed by, but later the year 1988, just before the big December school holidays, my grandpa came home from the council with good news.

My grandpa was my grandpa, always humble in everything he says and do, indeed he was an honorable man of faith, a man of his word and he loved his family, and his grandchildren to the outer, he always took his grandchildren out for nearby walks on daily basis, exploring adventures with him was also the most unforgettable and exited times, he even has teaches us how to make a bow and an arrow, how to make a guitar and banzo out of polish cans and wires, he told us everything about a farm yard and how to took care of it, how to make things work when it looked like it can not be used anymore.

He was indeed a man of many talents, I remember how he once took an empty twin saver tissue box that was eventually ready for the dust bin, but he took it and made for us a play television out of it, so that we could have a toy to play with, what an man of a super creativity, he was.

He was an awesome, and great man of faith, trying to fill the gap of an absent father in our lives, and he tried to fulfill his role as a grandparent too, I loved him, for who he was and what he did for us.

So he came home from the council, called the family together, early that night after everyone was at home and settled.

We used to have night gatherings at evening before the wooden stove under the candle light, because we did not have any electricity back then, we were always singing hymns and the family would encouraged one another with songs of praise to God, but this specific night, my grandfather did have something different to talk to us about, and he shared the news with us, that we are going to move from the farm to a place called Van Wyksvlei in the other side of town during the coming holidays of 1988, because the council eventually gave him a house after all the years that he was waiting on. It was the greatest news ever for our family, because for so long we stayed on a farm.

We were all very exited, from now on my mom was about to travel to work by bus or taxi and it will be a complete new thing and a new challenge for her.

And everything was going to be new and it's going to be an amendment for all of us. We moved into our new house in December 1988.

We were all really exited when we arrived in the area for the first time, the feeling of entering a new neighborhood, a new house with a bathroom and electricity in the house was just a feeling I could not actually described back then, because where we came from was no bathroom and no electricity at all.

And the house we stayed in on the farm was just a small house, we had one bedroom wich we divided into two rooms with a curtain, a kitchen, a living room and no bathroom at all,

This house was big enough, two bedrooms, a living room, a

kitchen and a bathroom, it was definitely more advanced like the one we came from.

The feeling was great and we could see many more people around us. On the farm there was only four houses, the one we stayed in, the house next to us on the farm was auntie Katriena and uncle Dyle's house where they stayed with their children and their children, then in the house on the end of the row we lived, stayed a big family, I remember auntie Sofie, auntie Syble, uncle Stemmer, Beryl, Sedick and their mom. The last house, was an alone standing house, in that house stayed auntie Sally and uncle Thomson with their two children, wich were Beryl and Basil and Beryl,'s daughter Salomie who I always played with as a kid, yes we had our moments and we do have memories, we were at the time around the same age.

They were one of the first families who had the privilege to moved from the farm.

So the year 1988 was also my last year at Pauw Gedenk Primary school at the age of nine, now I had to go back to Hillcrest Primary school where I started grade 4,(standard 2)as we called it back then those years. Hillcrest Primary school was the nearest school to the place we moved at. I was still a little boy with big dreams. I always had the dream to become a writer one-day, because I would sit hours with a pen and paper and just write, I even had my own diary back then, year after another, but I lost my information somehow along the way. I definitely had more than one God given talent inside of me, I was good at writing, drawing, painting, I also had the dream to play the piano, I loved to sing and there was so much more locked up inside of me, that I had to discover.

My new life, my new journey started in the year of 1989. I attended the new school. Eventually I started to make new friends with children my age in the area we moved to, they were also attending the same school I did.

One or two of my friends at home attended at other schools, also in our hometown. They were all nice and great friends indeed. I was getting older, during 1989 I became ten years old. I met a boy in the same class of mine who wanted to be my friend , but he was much different then me, yes he was also a child of a single mom , but he was not that well mannered, I gave it a go and never did I know that even his energy would have a big influence on my life.

He was a nice boy, but he lived in a complete different environment at home as I did.

Things were just not in place at their house,and everything was just out of order, and it did have a big impact on my life too, because we became friends.We used to walked together from school in the afternoons.

He came to school with books of naked models and then he would invite me to have a look at the books he brought from home, then he would do all kinds of fantasies with the books.

All of a sudden I was under this influence and negative energy. I was just a little too young to notice what really was really going on. It definitely destroyed my life in some way back then, because I would come home from school, take a book wich I received from him, go to a silent place and fantasize with it, just like he did and that power was building and growing in my life from day to day, and my spirit was definitely poisoned.

Later that year, my grandpa got sick, my mom was still working at the place she worked as hairdresser, like I said, at the hair salon in the town, located in Church street. My grandpa was diagnosed with some sort of cancer at the time and things started to not be the same anymore at home. The following year my mother ended her day job at the hair salon for another job at a can factory in Paarl, we used to call the place "Jones", originally "Langeberg Foodcan". So the struggle entered our house and my grandpa's illness became priority to the family. Surely it had a massive impact and influence on my attendances and my achievements at school and also I started to lack of going to my Sunday school.Sunday school was in town at the church and sometimes at the church hall called, the "Breedsaal".

I couldn't go anymore, because we started to have financial problems and to get to town i needed to take the bus or the taxi to drop me off at the bus-stop near the church, but there was no money to pay for the service.Our family became somehow very poor in everything we used to had.

I remember, coming from school with a hungry stomach day after day, and when I go to the bread tin, I only saw the empty plastic bags inside.

Things became much worse, now my mother's sister who was married to her husband together with her four children started to have problems in their household, her husband became an addicted alcoholic, and he sometimes got so angry that he started to be violent with them. So she moved out, along with her four children and they came and they stayed with us.. Now all of a sudden, the space in the house was getting smaller for all of us ,and the house environment also began to change.

We all, somehow got along with each other. My mother's younger sister also had a son, he was born in the time before we moved from the farm, his name was Nashwin. We were so impressed with him, because there was just something about him that made us all very happy.

Never the less, but the time passed by and we were all under one roof and we enjoyed each others company, we were always looking out for each other.

Then things take a next heat, my grandpa suddenly died. It was the most hurtful experience I ever had in my life, I knew that he was sick, I knew that he has been taking up in hospital for treatment, but no one ever told me that he was going to die.

I remember, my mom was coming from work at midday and her eyes was wiped in tears. Then I saw my two aunts screaming and crying around and it hurt me so much, because I didn't know any of this things could happen to my loving family.

The worse experience I ever had was to see my mom crying like a baby, and that broke me apart.

There was a funeral, my grandpa was lying in a wooden box and people were singing sad songs, all over the faces of the people around me were tears. I saw people, I never ever had seen in my life before and they were all sad. I tried to figure it out, but nothing made any sense to me at the time. After everything was done and the funeral was over, there was a calmness in the atmosphere and happiness came from somewhere, through again, people were eating and they were enjoying themselves in different conversations, I saw them put my grandfather to the ground, and I did not understand anything about what happened and why they had to do that, but I knew he was not coming back again.

The hurt of knowing that I did not have a biological father of my own and now my grandpa that was taking away from me, and the fact that it is going to be like forever, hurt me so much inside, I just sat aside from everyone else with a sad face and a broken heart.

The question that was popping in my head was, "I wonder if this is not maybe what happened to my dad I never knew?", then I started to answer my question all by myself, "that is maybe why my mother don't want to talk about it," can it be.?

I wondered.

So I had to ask my mother about this again, but her answer was just the same as it was before. So what really happened to my dad? who is supposed to be my father.

I never received the answer from my mother, because she didn't want to talk about it at all.

The damage was done, my heart was in a state of disaster and I had to search for answers. My heart was missing a part a piece of his own and the death of my grandpa was making the hole in my heart eventually bigger, because it hurts. And the fact that I was not the boy I used to be before, and the influence of another boy's behavior, and a sexual spirit that started to manifest in my Life, it made me so weak.

I was a very sensitive and soft child. I always had a smile on my face, but slowly and surely the smile I used to have was fading away.

One day after school as we gathered as cousins and playing in the house, our youngest cousin Nashwin, the son of my mother's baby sister was playing outside in the yard with his ball, while we were inside the house busy doing our homework, we were also supposed to kept an eye on him, because he was the youngest of us all at the time, our parents were at work and after the death of my grandpa, my grandma became bedridden

So we had to be on the look out for each other, but also to our grandmother who was bedridden.

Then we heard a sound of car wheels that screamed outside and a weird sound like a massive hit into an object.

We ran outside and there we saw our youngest nephew lying on the ground and his head was covered in blood.

He was run down by a car, while he was chasing after his ball.

It was just another tragic moment in my life, a moment that hurt me so much, because I personally could felt the quilt of knowing, we had to be on the watch out over our little one but we failed.

By the grace of God, he was not dead, but he was highly injured.

Slowly all the pain inside of this heart of mine started to grow at a fast paste.

Then something else happened, I had a friend who stayed three houses from us and he used to come after school to play at my house. This particular afternoon he came over and brought with him a wooden-made sword, he came over and he made for me also a sword, so we were going to play sword-sword, like we called it back then, then something happened, he took out his sword with the sharp edge and sharp point at the front of his sword and he pushed the sharp point of his sword with a great force at my private parts and my testicles got hurt. That pain was not anyone's hope for, I dropped down in pain. This friend of mine ran off to his parents house. That night I couldn't even sleep, I was crying in silence, night after night and I never told anyone up till today about the incident that happened. The next day my testicle went swelling for some long time, i just kept it silence and talked to nobody about it, not even my mother. As time went by I got used to it and the swelling went down all by itself and away, the pain slowly got lighter, but it always disturbed my mind, because I knew my private parts was not the same anymore and it might be damaged.

So another hurt was added on to me and the hole in my heart started to grow much more and the emotions I had was manifested somehow on my face.

Time passed by, my achievements on school dropped down to very low, I was not the child I used to be who pushed for the best in class and I knew it, because of the things that was happening to me, and it started to haunt me somehow. It was leading me into a direction I did not ask for.

I believe that God knew me, and it was God who allowed this things in my life.

Where will it end? I asked myself, but I didn't know. Where did it all came from? I couldn't imagine, but it happened somehow, but I have to search for the answers.

Too much hurt was troubling me from inside, and it was starting to eat me from inside. I was searching for answers.

Then, another incident happened, we used to have a porch at the backdoor of the house, the height from the ground up to the end of the wall of the porch was three meters. When you came out from the back door you would go down from the porch by stairs to enter the ground of the backyard. I went out the door and I played on the porch, somehow I leaned over on the edge of the wall of the porch, and out of no way, I just felt that something, lifted my legs from the ground, but I did not see anybody at all, there was no one, so I loosed balance and dropped three meters over the wall of the porch, down to ground. At that time the ground beneath was laid with concrete platform, so I dropped down and felt with my forehead to the concrete platform. For a moment I was out from this world in unconsciousness and nobody saw what happened at all. Back then I was eleven years old. My grandma was still alive, she was bedridden like I said ,and she was not able to get up from bed, so she was not in a state to look out for me at all.

Again I didn't tell anybody about what happened to me, my mother came home from work and she saw that my head was injured, she asked me about it, so I told her. I was not taking to any doctor or hospital, my injury once again all healed by itself, as the time went by.

Friday nights, was movie night at our house and we as children would be spoiled with pocket money from our parents on every Friday night, then we would ran off to the shop ,a nearby store named "Mr Sha's Corner" at the time and then we would get ourselves sweets , chips cool drink and whatever we needed to treat ourselves with for movie night. We had a small black and white television wich my mother bought from a furniture place in Paarl. Every Friday night we would sit down with the family and watch our favorite movies, Vendetta and Sending Vietnam.

One Friday, as we ran off to the shop around half past seven at noon, and the sun was already getting down, something else happened to me.

I remember it was summertime, the weather was hot outside and a light warm wind was blowing.

I was raised as a barefoot child, because of our circumstances, my mother and family didn't have the money to by us any shoes, so barefoot was my lifestyle till up to the day I went to high–school.

Yes for Sunday school I did have a pair of school shoes to wear, but other than that, I didn't know about shoes.

So we took off barefoot to the shop with our pocket money in hands.

As we got closer to the shop, all of a sudden my right feet started to burn like hell and my older cousin, Loretta the daughter of my oldest aunt, started to scream with a loud panic voice, "Shane you stepped on to a scorpion and there it goes that way!"

She saw everything that happened to me that evening.

My feet started to burn like hell, I started to scratch my feet on the sand and against the warm road with the hope that it would get better and that the burning feeling might go away, but it didn't in fact it increased.

I turned around and without going to the shop I took off and I ran back home.

As I ran home I started to feel very sick and weird, and the poison of the scorpion took over my entire body, my mind was getting in a confusing zone , my legs became lame and weak and I spoke things that doesn't make any sense to anybody.

At home my cousins told the family what happened, so my mother gave me medicine and she kept my foot in hot salty water, but I was so confused.

I went to sleep that night with a heart that was pumping like a car race , and in my mind I was so drunk of the poison, but God was with me and in it all.

What I can tell you up till today from that happenings of that day is, my life was never the same again.

I was poisoned by a scorpion and his poison was in my blood from that day, my life started to fall apart on a very fast paste.

Things unusual started to happen to me in my spiritual, physical and mental existence.

I was confused, the more I needed to move forward in that small life of mine, it fell that I moved backwards and I started to make bad choices and decisions in my daily life , and everyone who connected to my life were influenced. I even started to hurt my mom in many different ways and brought unhappiness and disappointments more often, and the hole in my heart was getting so much bigger than it was before, because I was not the same person anymore and my mother was also acting strange towards me, because of my works and deeds.

I was still on primary school, trying to managed and trying to kept my good habits and personality, but it brought disappointment on disappointment. During this time I found out that my biological dad was actually a man from another race, I also found out that I had another brother from another woman from my biological dad.

The years went by and in an wink of an eye I was in grade 7,(standard 5.) My brother was heading to primarily school too, as a grade 1, (sub A) learner at the school I was going to, for the last year on primary school, was it my duty to watch over my little brother because it was a complete new thing for him, and my mother still had that little bit of trust in me. For some reason I thought I had to play dad over my brother, because I was over protected to him, and I screwed up again, one day I came home from school, my brother was supposed to come home before I get home and yes he did, but when I came at home , he was not at home and I started to look for him all over. After sometime he came home and I asked him where he was, so he said that he was at his friend's house and they were playing, so I got angry and I took a thin orange pipe and started to hit him all over his body with it. That, I believe today was never necessary, it never had to happened, it happened because evil was taking my life over, I was not the same person anymore, my brother was only seven years old and I was thirteen years old at the time.Evil entered my life on this age, it was pure evil. I looked at my brother and I saw how the scars of the pipe was lying on his body and that made me so sad again ,and now my little brother was hurt and he was afraid to be around me. When our mother came home , she took that same pipe and started to gave me the lesson of my life.

Today I can tell you that it was the works of the devil that made me did something like that to my little brother, the devil is a liar, he always tries to break down what God has put together and what God made beautiful.

He who is the devil wanted to destroyed the bound between me and my brother and my mother and brought on hatreds, but God had his way of restoring things, Thank you my brother that you has forgiven me for the wrong I have done to you.

I was on high-school at Bergriver Secondary school also in Wellington. I turned fourteen in the year of 1994. Again it was a new start in my life, at secondary school life. And the searh for answers was eating me up inside.

A big part of me was already damaged, and it was getting bigger by the day. The hole in my heart was like an cold dark empty room.

Word of encouragement:

Mathew 7:7

Ask, Seek, Knock

Ask and it will be given to you; seek and you will find; knock and the door will be opened to you.

2 Corinthians12:9

But he said to me, "My grace is sufficient for you, for my power is made perfect in weakness." Therefore I will boast all the more gladly of my weaknesses, so that the power of Christ may rest upon me.

23

Chapter3

Direction and choices:

In December 1993, it was registration time at Bergriver Secondary High school in Wellington, time for the new grade 8(standard 6) learners to have their registrations done.My mother somehow managed to give me the registration school fees for the coming year.

My older cousin Loretta, was also a learner at the school at the time. Registration day was on a Saturday in December month in 1993. Early the morning of the existing day me and her took off to school,to get our registrations done.

We went to school payed the registration fees, then we headed home again to enjoy the holidays.

Holidays went by and now we were ready for the coming school year.

My mother somehow managed to bought me a pair of black school shoes, a white school shirt, a grey school trouser and I even received a new backpack and a school tie from one of my family members.

First day at school was great, once again I met some nice people, all surrounded with new faces I was.

Then I made friends with a boy called Jeremy, he was a little of a bit older than me, but we were in the same classroom.

Jeremy was a very nice and friendly person and he was also a very sensitive boy, but he was a cigarette smoker.

Me was not a cigarette smoker at all, yes I did try to do it one or two times on primary school, but it didn't work out for me in any way. This time things were different, I became weak to the temptation coming my way. Jeremy was the one who came to school with lots of cigarettes, because he was a mergin on the school premises and he would sell the cigarettes to other learners. To me he was more like a father figure, because he was older than me and he was always looking out for me and concerned about how I was doing, he always gave me things that my parent couldn't afford to give to me, sometimes when I don't had any food at school, he was the one person who would gave his lunch box to me.

On high-school I saw something else, I saw that every second boy I looked at, had an ear ring pierced through their ears, so I decided to follow their lead, just to fit in to the high school lifestyle at high school.

Jeremy was the one who introduced me to cigarette smoking and how to do it the right way. After the normal style of smoking cigarettes he decided that we had to upgrade our style of smoking, so, he brought to school a broken bottle-head, then he filled up the broken bottle-head with broken and crushed cigarettes then we would go somewhere peaceful on the school premises and smoke it. Everyday, during our breaks at school we went behind the school building and do our smoking thing, we called it a cigarette pipe. Not very long after that experience we had another upgrade, we started to fill the bottle pipe with marijuana. Exactly how I got into my drug problem, I was introduced by a friend on an early stage of my life to drugs. It became a hobby of mine and a very bad habit in my life.

I started to do things I never did before.

Things were now really starting to get out of control in my life.

I remember how I was hunted by two brothers , they were twins. They were actually from another school in the area, so they started to chase after me for no reason, everyday I had to run from school to escape them and the situation went on for like more than a year, somehow they gave up on chasing me and they dropped out of school. I was in grade 8 at school at the time, things were getting hot and out of control for me,even at home.

At home I was friends with a much older guy then me, because he was also a marijuana pipe smoker and I had to be friends with someone who was doing what I was busy doing. The friends I used to be friends with at home in Van Wyksvlei was no longer my friends anymore because of my bad habits.

I was also in relationship with a girlfriend a year younger than me during that time, her name was Lucrecia, she had the most beautiful personality I couldn't resist, but because of my bad habits , I had to gave her up, because l believed she did not deserved someone like me at all anymore. I didn't want her to be upset or in anyway unhappy or hurt, because of my bad decisions I have made, so I gave up on her.I just fell that I had done to many things wrong and it would not be fair of me to brought someone like her under that negative energy I was influenced with.

I chose to be friends with this older person, his name was Petro, he was turning 20 years of age at the time. He used to listen to reggae music and he was a big fan of Bob Marley.

I also learned how to use alcohol during the time, because he sometimes drank alcohol and we would do it together. Things for me started to get rough. Many times we ended up in fights and arguments with other guys. We acted like gangsters, we also walked with knifes in our pockets to protect ourselves from danger.

The years was passing by, I joined a team at school, they were called The Anakies, I started to wear black rubber zombies on my risks, I started to read books of the religion of satan, because the Anakies was a satanic cult. I took the religion and culture home into the environment I lived in and I started to practice it at home. I definitely became vulnerable to the challenge under the power of a satanic cult. While I joined the cult, I was also part of gangs in our neighborhood, first I was part of the Peacemakers then I became a Casanova boy.

But my mind was deep into the satanic cult, I studied the culture and religion, their secret words, the colors and even the way they dress and how they write their words.

I sold my soul to the devil on a very early stage of my life, because of the hurt and unforgiveness I carried along in my heart, because of the disappointments and the self blame in my heart. It definitely ruled my life. I was so deep into the cult, that I started to burn my own flesh with cigarette buts, I cut myself with blades and started to ate crushed glass from time to time. That satanic power took my life over by force, I couldn't control myself. From my friends who witnessed it back then and knows about all the happenings in my life is still alive today.

I went through hell, from a loving, kind and happy child to a complete unhappy, hateful and inhuman monster.My mother and family did not understood me anymore at all, because evil was taking over my life.

All the things that happened to me had an influence on my family. My family was not the same anymore. I remember, we as children used to play together and we were so bound to each other, but then things changed and we were not the same anymore.

Hatred and violence entered our house, we were arguing for no monetary reason with each other and the damage was done. We all had some dreams and hopes for the future and we could always discussed it with one another, but all of it just disappeared.

My one nephew went to army and he was away for two years, when he came back from his service, nothing was the same at home anymore. Everything has changed, and I know that it must have set him back in life too, because he didn't expect any of the things that he came upon.

I started to get addicted to the drugs, marijuana and alcohol I used.

During that time, my mother got a job offered from Miss Theron, she was the co-owner of a printing company named Boland Press in Wellington, her husband was the owner. Miss Theron used to go to the hair salon where my mother worked in earlier years, and my mother became Miss Theron's personal hair dresser.

My mother was never a drinker at all, she started to drink beer and I believe that started because she did not know what to do anymore about me who gave her ups and downs, because of the stress and depression she was going through. Every weekend she became not herself anymore, she had a friend, our neighbor and they would enjoy themselves over every weekend. Later time, my mom's older sister started to join them too, and it went chaos. They started fighting and arguing. My mom's older sister who was still married to her husband then became pregnant on her age, from another young man in the neighborhood, under the influence of alcohol. She was still married but not with her husband anymore. I remember that her other children started to hate her for what she did to them, and it did had an enormous effect on them, because they did not expect anything like that from their mother at all. They were much disappointed. They really hated her for what she did, they even hated the father of the baby, and they spoke words against them that the see would not cleanse them at all. Everything was just falling apart.

We as children used to get pocket money from our parents, our moms but they stopped it all, because of our behavior.

I then decided to steal from them. I was always on the look out for their handbags and purses and then I would help myself when I found it.

My mom somehow figured out that I stole from the house, and she eventually cut me from everything in the house. They labeled me as a thief and I started to believe that I am one.

So know I became a thief also. Weekends we went out clubbing, I got by times involved with fights and arguments, because I was operating like a gangster like I said.

Late at nights or early morning hours I would come from my so called lifestyle, while everyone else was asleep, I would came from my nice times and knock like a police officer on my family's door so that they had to open up for me, because I want to sleep. I became rude and rebellion. My cousins and nephews, they started to do the same.

Time went by, during the year of 1995, I eventual quit school.

I quit school, because of the things I allowed to possessed my life, I quit school because, I couldn't function like a normal child anymore.

I quit school because of my lifestyle, bad habits and the needs in my life.

I started to stand on the corners of the streets and on the sidewalks of shops to ask and beg for money.

My mother's younger sister

was the silent one, but she started to speak up against the things that was happening in the household.

She saw what was happening, she was not talking it good in anyway, but I believe that she have had seen enough. She and my mother end up in a fight,and their relationship as close sisters was no more.

My mother's drinking habit, my aunts drinking habits, my rebellion lifestyle, my cousins and nephew's wrongs and rude manners, she couldn't handle it anymore.

My grandmother like I said was still alive, but she was bedridden. She placed the house into my mother's baby sister name, because she was the only sober person from the family. Sarah(Santie) was her name.

Sarah, met a man as her partner in her life. At first we as children did not want to accept him, and we had some arguments with him and some leaded to fights and rude acts, but time passed by and they got married.

Out of their marriage was born a son named Gershwin. They had two sons, remember Nashwin the one who was in the incident with the car, and then Gershwin.For us as a family things has really changed. Life was never the same again.

Word of encouragement:
James 1:5

He gives us the gift of free will so that we can make decisions and choose to love him. Which means we also have to make these earthly decisions. He doesn't leave us unequipped, and we can ask him for guidance and wisdom for these choices.

Chapter 4

The Wrong but Right:

I dropped out of school during the middle of the year of 1995, I was in grade 9 (standard 7). I started to follow the life of a gangster.

Things began to get much worse than it ever was before in my life, I was only 16 years old, but I already lived my life like an adult in person. All the wrong things like Sex, drugs and alcohol became my daily bread and breath.

I had no spiritual connection with God at all in my life, to me spiritual life with God didn't exist anymore, I served satan and all his lies. I had a couple of drinking buddies in my life and we used to have a close relationship with each another. While I was out on the streets to hustle, I always saw older men and father figures to their families, as they came from work on daily basis, I looked at them and I always said to myself, "one day I am going be like them".

One thing that has triggered my mind about them was, on Fridays I saw the men in our neighborhood came from their day tasks,each from different jobs, then they would buy groceries and clothes for their families from their own pockets, like all grown men used to do.

Sometimes I saw some of them would go to the shebeens and bought cases of beer for themselves from money they worked for. Somehow I desired to be like them and to go and work for my own money.

It definitely triggered my mind me and took my attention away, that I want to be like them one day.

Something else happened during that year 1995. One of the men in the neighborhood who used to work at a local hardware shop in town, came to me and he told me that the shop he was working at is looking for young people to help out at the store. He invited me to come and see if there was any chance for me to get in.

The Monday morning I went down to the shop and quest what, The boss of the store came to the doorway while I was standing at it, he asked me who I was and I told him in answering his question. When he heard my name he took me by the hand and said to me, "Your name is already here , you just wait here,someone will come and show you where you must take your position in"

I felt so good and impressed about what I heard, because for so long I hoped that someone might come my way and show me that he cares.

Thanks to the man from my neighborhood, Ivan was his name,because he has sorted out everything to the boss on behalf of me. I just needed to show up.

At noon I went home from my first day at work and I told my family at home about the good news.

My mom responded: "I hope you look after your job" I was hoping that things might change for the good at home now that I have a job, but it didn't.

My past was following me everywhere I go. At work, the

people were all so nice and friendly to me, but my bad habits disappointed me and it disappointed my family more and more and all the people who were connected to me.

We worked on a fortnight scheme at the hardware store and we were supposed to be paid every second Friday.

The first week went by and it went great, but the second week. I received a job description as a shelf packer and the test was heavy on me, because I was working with all kinds of expensive stuff right in front of my eyes that I may could benefit from.

I started to steal from the shop. I only worked at the store for that two weeks. The quilt I felt in my heart made me quit my job, I disappointed that man who was trying to help me, so I failed the test.

Today I know that it was a chance given by God, wich I couldn't recognized at that time, but I know, at least all my human feelings were not dead at all, because I felt the quilt in my heart and that means that somewhere out there has to be hope for me.

At home people were not happy about what I did it all, then I received another job from my neighbour who lived next door to me, he worked at a bakery in Paarl. A week after I left the hardware store, I went with my neighbour who was an adult, his name was Patrick , he was also the son of auntie Sally and uncle Thomson who used stay with us on the farm in the alone-standing house, wich I talked about earlier. I started to work with him at the bakery, also for one week, something happened at the bakery.

One of the day workers, clothes were stored in his locker at the bakery, the locker was not locked, so I opened it up and I saw a pair of shoes(grasshoppers) in the locker.

I took it from the locker, put it in my bag and the next morning after I arrived at home from work, I started to burn and polished the shoes wich I took from the locker.I took a very hot spoon wich I burned the shoes with , because it was brown and sweight, I gave it a smooth finished and in Tony red colour. The next night shift I decided not to go with my neighbour to the job again, so he went alone, and when the morning arrived he came back from work and he asked me, "listen did you took shoes from a locker at work, you have to give it back to me, and you don't have to come to work again," he said.

I responded and reply, "No I didn't took anything", I lied to my neighbour, than he said to me, "It never happened before in the bakery, why now that you were there."

Then he added, by saying, "and the man, the owner of the shoes is coming personal to you today after work."

The man was working a day shift.

Later the day he came by, I never met him before because he was on day shift and I was supposed to be on night shift. He was a black African guy, he came by with one of the bakery's trucks, because he was also the truck driver at the time, He then asked me about the shoes, and if I somehow took it from his locker, I went to him at the truck he came with and I told him everything, "yes I did" I replied and told him that I was really sorry about what I did. He accepted my apologies

Time went by, my life was still a mess, nobody could trust me anymore, and my past kept on following me where ever I went.

Things at home was in a state of complete disaster for me and the rest of my family.

In 1996, September month I received another job offer and this time from my neighbour on the other side of the fence, he was a cabinetmaker at a company called Prowell woodworkers also located in Wellington.

On a Friday he called my aunt over the fence and told her that the company was looking for people.

My aunt told me about it, the next morning, it was Saturday and I went to the factory and I was getting a job.

We worked that Saturday till twelve o clock midday.

The foreman on the job came to me and said, "you must come back on this coming Monday again and bring your identity book with you".

And from that day I worked at the furniture company. We specialized in the making of all office furniture , bedroom and kitchen cupboards.

They gave me permanent job at the company after I contracted for three months, then I became a permanent worker and I worked for 22 years at the company. A lot happened during that time. I never knew that I was so skill fulled and many of my talents were born during the 22 years.

I went home that first Saturday and I told my mom and the family again that I have a job again.

Nobody said anything, because they thought that I was in any way going to mess it up again, so they just kept themselves quiet.

I didn't messed it up, but my life took another journey,

I stopped with the drugs and I stopped with the marijuana smoking, but I became an addicted alcoholic.

Alcohol became the controller of my life. From time to time I will take a marijuana cigarette to have a smoke, but I did not make it a regular thing like I used to.

Alcohol made me do things I did not cared about at all,when I had to be in work on a Monday then I would rather stay at home. I did not gave any money to my mother at all, because of the bad habit I had with the alcohol.

My lifestyle became as an entertainer to others.

My mother met a person, who worked also at the printing company where she worked at, so they became interested in one another and started a relationship. His name was Denvor.

I did not like it at all , because I don't need any man in my life who wants to play dad to me and my brother, so I started to build grudges against the idea and I hated what my mom was doing.We had lots of fights and misunderstandings and things were getting worse. My mother somehow decided to wrote me off.

She treated me back then like if I was not her child anymore.

My brother on the other hand was never like me, He was still at school and she tried to make the best that she could to safe him from getting to where I ended up.

Nobody really knew how I felt inside, my heart was damaged, I was cold, I was hurt, disappointing, ashamed and I was missing a piece of my heart that I just could not find.

My mother's sister ,Sarah (Santie) was on the verge of breaking down, she made her mind up, she

and her husband, Shaun decided that "enough is enough" and that things could not go on like this.

I think what they must have thought was, that they are not going to rise their child or children under the circumstances and influences we were in.

They decided to give us all notice and we had to go and look for a place where we could stay and sleep completely on our own.

They went to the attorneys, asked and received a letter from them and gave it to my mom and my mom's older sister. My mom's older sister went staying with the young man wich see was pregnant from, she took with her, two of her children and she carried the one in labour, the other two children needed to find there own way.

Me, my mother and our little one then stayed at the house of a friend of mine, in the same street we used to live in. Then one of the children from my aunt did not find any place to stay so he came and lived with us. We stayed at my friend's family, it the last house on the corner of Bailey Avenue in Van Wyksvlei, our family house was down the road at number 20 Bailey Avenue.

At the time we stayed at my friend's house, my friend stayed right over the road with other people in Carterville (Egoli) where he boarded.

His mother , stepfather , biological father and his sister with her kids stayed in the house of his, and then we moved in together with them.

He went away from home because he got converted and born again and didn't want to be in an environment like it was back at home.

We stayed for some time there together with his family.

Things were not that good there.

In the house was the stepdad of his and also his biological father, but his mom was not attracted to his biological dad anymore, they lived as if they never had something in common.

While staying there my drinking habit became a daily thing.

Everyone in the house was alcohol drinkers and they were massive drinkers.

When they get drunk, violence always came out of no way and people will fight and arguing.

So I decided to sleep there during the week and on weekends I slept at a shebeen, four houses from them.

I became like a house child at the shebeen during that time.

I also helped with selling the alcohol on weekends and on

Monday mornings I would go straight from the shebeen to my workplace at Prowell woodworkers.

Life was getting tough and difficult for me day by day.

After some time my mother decided that she is going to move with her boyfriend completely to the other side of the town, where he was from.

He lived in the place called Voordorp (Ghostown).

Voordorp is a place very near to the farm wich we used to lived, before we moved to Van wyksvlei.

It was based around the school's and places where I walked as a kid from home to school on 6-9 years old.

Many of the people in the area knew my mother very well.

So she moved to Voordorp to her boyfriend's house, it was actually his grandmother and grandfather's house, but they were already laid to rest and the children lived in the house. So it happened that my mother just took of to work one morning and she never came back to my friend's house where we stayed.

She arranged with the taxi driver, who drove my brother to school and home to drop him off at the address where she would be.

She just left me, without saying anything and suddenly I was out there, really all by myself.

Yes I was still working, I didn't treat her like a son had to treat a mother at all. My nephew the oldest son of my mother's older sister was with me in the same situation.

So my friends mom, told us that she was not going to give us a place to stay anymore we must go find a place somewhere else to stay.

I did have a work to go to, but I did not have any place to stay at, my money went out to all the wrong things in life.

Every Friday I had to pay the mergins at the shebeens for the week's credits wich I took on account.

So after some time I heard from people where my mom was moved at and I decided to go there and have a word with her, but it did not help me in any way, she didn't want me there at all.

So I slept for the last time at my friend's house and early the next morning I went to work, without any food, as the day went by I made up mind , I went to my old house where my auntie Sarah was at and had a talk with her, I asked her to give me a another chance, I explained that, "I am homeless and I do still have a work and I will give to her money every end of the week for my stay, I shall try my best to become better." It was all empty promises I made to her.

So after a long talk she said, "alright we are going to give you a chance, as long as you stay under our rules".

I stayed for only a week, she gave me a place to stay, she put in food for me for work, washed the only clothes I had on my body and even gave me clothes from her husband to wear and I still messed it up again.

The Friday wich were pay-day arrived and I was no where to be found.

I went that weekend to the place where my mother stayed, they let me in only for the weekend and I drank out every single sent of my hardworking money. I was careless.

The Monday I went from there to work, but when the noon of the Monday arrived, I had to find a place to stay again. I was all alone out in the world on my own.

My mother thought I was going back to her sister's place because I told her I was staying with my aunt.

I had no way to go, at all I lied to her, because I didn't kept the promise I've made to my aunt.

So I end up on the streets at the age of 17 years old, in 1997 without any place to put my head to sleep.

The cold ground and the cold grass became my bed and the stones was my pillow.

I remember my first night out on my own, I found myself exhausted ,tired hurt and sad on the sport ground of Weltevrede , Van Wyksvlei, on the B-field, sleeping without anything to cover me with. And I put myself down on the grass beneath the rugby posts.

And that was my bed outside in a world I never knew before and I didn't asked for this results I had to faced.

Word of encouragement:

Proverbs 24:16

For a just man falleth seven times, and riseth up again: but the wicked shall fall into mischief.

Romans 8 38

38 For I am convinced that neither death nor life, neither angels nor demons, neither the present nor the future, nor any powers, 39 neither height nor depth, nor anything else in all creation, will be able to separate us from the love of God that is in Christ Jesus our Lord.

Chapter 5

The Break point:

I ended up frustrated, angry, unhappy and rude.

People gave me different type of names. They labeled me. At night I was sobbing from all the sadness in my heart.

Some people didn't want to be in my space or presence because of my behavior.

I became a very violent young man, because of the frustrations in my head, and the hurt deep down in my heart. I always hoped that things would get better some day.

I was indeed a hard worker at the factory I worked, regardless who I became.

I always had the ability to learn from others.

I started to work as a sander at the furniture factory, and my foreman and employer was happy with my work and what I did at work.

So as the time went by I had some "in house training" and "different courses."

I went back to where my mother was staying at the time, because I had no other place to stay, so she took me in with her.

First I slept outside in the back yard, then I've been invited to come and sleep inside the house with the landlord, George.

My mother and her boyfriend slept in a very very small room wich was attached to the house, it used to be a tool room.

In the room was only space for a bed, a shelf where they could put their clothes on, and a radio where they played there favorite songs from.

The only space left that they could use in the room was right in front of the bed and it was as wide as the length of a ruler.

I slept inside the house of the landlord who was back then the uncle of my mother's boyfriend.

Me and him became good friends, he was a guitarist and I really liked that part of his story, because I loved singing, so he would play and I would sing a song, and that made me discover that I somehow do have potential inside of me. I was not that good of a singer at all, but I could sing.

Weekends after weekends we were partying and then we made music while we were partying.

My drinking problem was on another level and when I became drunk I became rude.

I became violent and I could not stand people who irritates me at all.

Sometimes old friends from Van Wyksvlei where we used stay would come and visit me, because some of them also started to work at the place I was working at.

One of them had a legal pistol, because he was a security at the time.

One day I grabbed his pistol and I just started to shoot around like a crazy man. Luckily for me no one was injured or dead at all, but damages were made to the landlords ceiling.

I thought people might call the police, but no one did, so yes I was lucky. I became an uncontrollable freak.

I turned 18 years old and I already worked for a year at the factory. As the time went by I became a little calm.

That for me was a bonus on my journey and definitely a good sighn for me, so there have to be hope for the future somehow.

My past kept on following me wherever I went, too much things was stock up in my heart and it all started back then when I was just a little boy around the age of six.

The hurt was eating me up from inside and in someway it manifest in the natural life I lived.

So what was the plan of God according to my life, because to me life did not make any sense at all anymore.

I remember the one time I went out of control and I break a window of the house where I stayed with a brick and they called out the police for me.

They arrested me and on the way to the police station on my way to the prison cell, a police officer came from no way up to the officers who was taking me to the prison cell, and he said to them, "There is no need to go and lock him up anymore, you can leave him now", then he added by saying "while you were on your way to the police station, someone came in and pay for his fine of arrest".

That for me was something else, so they unlocked the hand–cuffs around my hands and they let me go.

And life started to turn around for me somehow.

I did not understand anything of it at all and it always had me thinking about that moment. Someone came in to the police station and paid a fine for me back then.

Today I totally understand everything, It was God who sent an angel to buy me out of prison. I know it may sounds funny to some people , but it is the pure truth, and God Himself is thy witness. I never ever heard of the person again.

That was my first experience about an angel, I didn't saw him back then, never heard about him again, but I heard how the officers talked about him, and he didn't want the police officers to know who he was, so he introduced himself to them as "anonymous."

God allowed me to go through all of the bad things in life, I don't want you to get me wrong, I never blamed God at all, but he allowed me to be tempted by satan because He knew what He had in mind. He knew what I could handle and what I couldn't handle. Like we all somehow go through stuff and we start questioning God, but we go through stuff so that He can be Glorified, and somehow everything we went through is our anointing in our testimonies, to go out in the world and tell someone about how great He really is. Because our testimonies can safe another person's life and for God's purpose we can safe a soul from ending up in the wrong place.

Then something very beautiful happened to me,

The boyfriend of my mother had a cousin and she used to come and visit at the house where we stayed, because it was also her grandparent's house. I really liked her from the first time I saw her.

So we met, she was a bit older than me but I could felt that there was definitely that special connection between us. So it happened that we fell in love to each other. Things started to change for me and it was definitely pushing me into a whole new direction in life. A direction I never knew could exist for me in life, I was so used to all the bad things that happened in my life, I lost my hope in the good side of life.

So we got together and we spent times with each other more than anything else.

She became also friends with my mother and they understood

each other very well and liked each other's company very much.

From time to time she would take a drink but only on weekends and special occasions.

Yes she was a heavy drinker sometimes, but she did it with style, she could control herself and her situation. I never went to their house before, because I knew back then that people would have there thoughts about me. Everyone in the area knew my lifestyle back then.

But God always has His way of doing and dealing with things, He allowed things to happen.

A year passed by.

In 1999 something unusual happened, I was torched with the thought in my mind, that I will never be able to conceive a child to life, because of the injury to my testicle when I was younger, and that thought was one of the things who haunted my mind and it definitely broke me inside, it followed me everywhere I went, but somehow I took faith and I prayed to God and told him about how I felt inside. I told Him that I want to be sure about my situation, and I told God that if He is going to help me in my condition and make the impossible possible for me, then will radically change my life, and try to follow Him. I made a promise to God.

Yes, that was the prayer from my heart, and the tears rolled over my cheeks like never before. I was still a sinner under the power of the world and the satanic possession, but I turned in prayer against it all, because I remembered what I once were, where I actually came from and what I once heard and it stroked my mind, somewhere deep in my heart is a place where I came from because the foundation was laid upon my life when I was just a small boy, because I was baptized in the power of the Father ,son and holy spirit , I turned to that promise and after some time my girlfriend felt pregnant.

God has heard my prayer. I thought to myself, How could this be. Once again God showed up to me, although I was a sinner.

Life was slowly turning for me, but something weird started to happen to me after my girlfriend felt pregnant, My girlfriend's name was Karen, and she actually become my wife, but before we reach that side of the story let me just tell you what happened next.

I thought to myself, How could this be. I thought I couldn't conceive any child, but God heard my prayer, it felt like, God showed up to me and made His face shine upon me.

Life was slowly turning for around for the good me ,and satan on the other hand was never satisfied in what I did at all, because I turned my back on him and I started to look at God through the little faith that God kept safe in my heart, through everything I went through and satan became angry at me, because of what I did in prayer to God. Remember I told you that I sold my soul to the devil on an early age of my life and all of a sudden I changed on him and pray to the God the creator of heaven and earth, the big name who was and is and is to come.

So he got angry with me and he created an event to destroy my life, so he used every bad thing I ever done before and wich I took part of and he used it against, from the cigarettes up in the row including sex and drugs and he invited me through friends to join this end of year event away from home.

I went on this trip with the friends from work, without knowing what is going to happen, the plan that satan had in mind was to destroy me once and for all, so this day I took advantage from everything that was available at the event, suddenly I went blank and I had an overdose of the things I took. My mind stripped and I started to act like a was zombie, by times I just ran off like a headless fowl.

The next day I was so possessed in my mind and body, I've never ever felt this way in my life before, and fear overwhelmed my mind, and I became so afraid of the world around me and the world I was living in, I felt depressed, alone, afraid and stressed out, and he made me see things and faces that does not exist, he created an illusion in my head ,I started to hear voices in my head and people that laughed at me and he made me believe that I'm not worth it anymore. He created an illusion that did not exist. A spirit of quilt and self-blame came over me and I started to ran off to the hoods away from home where I stayed at. I was so confused, and afraid and alone.

With a baby on the way, given by God, the satan was not satisfied about it at all.

I ran off and he forced me into the direction of Van Wyksvlei, remember it was exactly where I started to worship him and practiced his cult, so he took me back there, I walked like a mad man over to my families place, and the only thing he made me to believe was that I have to end my life because I was not worthy to live anymore, and a suicide spirit came over me.

In my head he attacked, and he said to me, "you are going to sleep at your aunts house, and at midnight you take off , go to the train track and throw yourself underneath." What a liar he was.

So I did not have any control over everything that was happening to me, but God was planning something else.

At midnight I woke up like a mad man, I was sleeping on a mattress in the sitting room of my aunt that specific night, in front of the television, the television was switched on, he used the television as a demonic door of force and communication channel to get to me , I remember the sounds that came from the television sounded like they were talking and screaming and sending out thousands of horses to come and arrest me and kill me.

My aunts husband was also sitting in front of the television and I did not even knew that he was still watching television.

I woke up screamed like an animal and I started acted weird, and he made me saw at twelve at night demons trying to grab me, they wanted to arrest me. I was so afraid and nervous and I acted not normal.

I remember, aside on a small table wich was standing all alone was lying a bible , it was my aunt's bible , he made me grab the bible and I pulled the bible apart and it was turned in half.

Deep inside of my heart, God was acting on behalf of me, and in the spiritual world His angels stepped in for me, and they was fighting this evil.

Just like in the time of Job, when God said to the satan, "you can do whatever you want with Job, but his soul belongs to me."

God definitely had a plan all worked out with my life, and He knew that one day I will be saved.

He knew what He made me from, what I am about to handle and I what I could not handle.

So the devil made me vomited, and the outcome was blood like dark jelly, he made me vomited things I don't want to mansion in this book, but he did it.

My aunt called the neighbour at the Fortuins's house, right next to our house, a man I always had a really great big respect for.

He was a priest at the New Apostolic church where he attended. He came over and started to pray for me and all of a sudden things became calm. I remember , he said to me, "Declare with your mouth that God is almighty" and I did declare it several times.

MY aunt then phoned my mother, and she came from Voordorp over all the way to Van Wyksvleiwhere my aunt lived, in the middle of the night. Hours went slowly by and they wanted to take me at that time to a man who was a sangoma in the area. They wanted to hear from him what happened to me and how he could help me, but I responded and said, "No, I don't want to go there I am fine". I took the faith and I believed that God was on my side.

All of this happened on a Saturday night at midnight, morning hours.

Sunday morning they took me home, but at the afternoon I started to walk away from home again, this time I ended up in a place called Wolwekloof in the mountains near to Ceres. It was a camping resort back then.

We as friends used to go there in earlier days and it was located in the mountains near to "Ceres."

Somehow satan carried me away to the place called Wolwekloof on that specific day after we came from the incident at my aunt's house, I do not know much how I got there, but when I realized and came to my awareness somehow I found myself in that place called Wolwekloof, between the bushes,

what I do remember is that I felt exhausted and so powerless and then I dropped with my face straight on to the ground and my forehead fell on a solid rock, it looked like a paving but it was a rock.

Then I was unconscious for some time, I came back from the sleep and I felt the warm blood running over my face and and I looked down to the t-shirt I was wearing and it was covered in blood.

I was in a confusing state, and my head felt heavy, and also dizzy.

I stood up, pulled myself together and a started to walk.

All covered in blood. I started to walk, not knowing where I was headed to, but I just walked, I came to a road, then I saw people driving by, but no one even looked my way, for me it felt like they couldn't see me at all. My eyes were as big as saucers in my head, as I was told to after some time.

I pushed on.

Something unusual and strange happened to me on that day.

God send and angel to me, his figure looked like my deceased grandfather, I saw my granddad down the road dressed in all blue.

He was walking on his walking stick, on his head was the hat he used to wear and he walked, very very slow.

Sometimes, it looked like he stood still then he looked back into my direction, and it looked like he was watching if I was coming to him.

A voice spoke to me and said, "follow him" so I did.

He led me out of the bushes , the unknown territory towards the main road side who leads back to Wellington, he made sure that the distance between me and him, so that the distance was kept. I tried to walk faster so that I could catch up with him, but I couldn't get anywhere nearer to him.

All of a sudden he just disappeared.

Then the second encounter happened. I looked up and down the road to see if anyone was near to help me from the situation I found myself in, but there was no one.

I went to a couple of small houses, wich I saw from the road side for help, but they couldn't help me.

And the people was acting strange towards me and it felt to

me, like they were somehow afraid of me, so I slowly but surely pushed by moving forward. I was very tired, I needed help, I needed a doctor because I could feel that it was just a matter of time and I was not going to make it, I felt too exhausted and dizzy.

Something happened, God then did it again, this time a car came by, very slowly and stopped a distance in front of me. My help came from the Lord. I could feel that this was not any normal situation, I could sense that this was my help, this was ment for me.

The car came to stop, from a distance in front of me, while I walked towards the car, I just had this strange feeling, because nobody was coming out from the car.

Nobody was trying to come and ask how or if they could help me. Very-very strange, when I get to the back of the dark blue car , the right hand side back door just popped open and with out any words or conversation I just climbed into the car, because I didn't had any other choice.

Word of encouragement:

God brings us through breaking points, so that He may bring us to the blessing point.

Ephesians 4:26-27

"Don't let the sun go down while you are still angry, for anger gives a foothold to the devil."

Psalms 147 3?

3 He healeth the broken in heart, and bindeth up their wounds.

Chapter 6

The turning point:

So I got into the car, inside the car was this unusual presents, something I never ever experienced before, something like a presents of calmness, silence and a peace wich definitely was not from this world.

Suddenly I felt so comfortable and save inside of the car.

My head was still feeling heavy and dizzy and it felt like I was drunk, but it was not an usual drunk feeling.

On the back seat of the car on my left hand side was sitting a boy, he also looked like an adult, like someone I saw before, but I must have mistaken myself somehow, he was just sitting there, without saying anything but starring through the window of the car to the world outside.

On the front seats of the car sat two unusual persons, they were wearing soft linen in the colour of black and white, their faces was light skinned and shiny, their eyes were covered with dark sunglasses wich was tight on their faces just like the eyes of the bees.

They were not talking to each other and they did not even talked to me either, they just kept silence in the harmony of peace.

One was a male and the other was a female.

In the car, I remember, that the radio was playing, but it was not the normal radio station that we used to know, the music that played from the radio was no sound from this world, it sounded more like angels singing in one accord. All of a sudden the radio changes its channels and I heard a man with a deep voice spoke through the radio to me.

I couldn't talk back, because I was not capable of talking back in anyway.

As the voice spoke to me I listened to everything he said to me and it was as clear as daylight.

He was talking so much things, and I didn't understand what was going on. He talked to me about everything that has happened to me over the past years.

Today I am completely aware about what He talked to me about and what happened to me back then.

It was God who communicated to me through a channel of a radio in an unusual car.

The persons who drove the car was His angels who He sent out to reach for me and to rescue me from my situation and disaster and they took care of me.

What an experience it was, just another powerful encounter with God and the angels of heaven.

At first I did not believe anything that was happening to me, because it seemed so unreal, but it also felt somehow real, As the time went by God himself told me and revealed to me about that day, and what actually happened.

While we were driving, I became unconscious in the car and while I was in a very, very deep sleep He showed me an open field, the grass of the field was dry and in a state of disaster, exactly how my life was before the encounter with God, I saw how I lied on the open field, ready to die and the birds of the air prepared themselves to come and eat my flesh. In the middle of the field was standing an cow covered in blood, and flies was all over the blood.

Then I woke up, and I saw the car was driving up into the road where I lived, the car stopped on the corner of the street where I lived , they dropped me off at the corner and again without saying anything. Those people did not speak any word at all to me, they were just communicating with its others in eye contact.

I then get out of the car and I walked from the car towards our gate side at home, not more than 9 steps away from the car was the house, As I get to the gate, I turned around to say thank you with a hand swing, but the car was gone, "That can not be", I thought to myself, "I just walked over the road, how can it be that they drove so fast away"? I asked myself in my mind.

So I made it to home safely and secure.

I was staying at the time with my mother , her boyfriend Denvor, her uncle George and the others family members of them who lived their.

When I came inside to the yard , my mother looked at me and immediately she noticed that I was not in any good state at all.

The neighbours, they all came then over to the house and everyone was so concerned about me, and they wanted to know what happened to me. I couldn't explained to anyone anything that happened to me, but as my mother knew from the incidents that happened the night before, she noticed something must have happened again.

She called the police and the ambulance, the police then came fast enough and they took me to the police station, they t contacted the ambulance, at the police station we waited for the ambulance to arrive, I was in a unbelievable confusing state , the ambulance arrived and they put me inside on the bed. Like I said I was in a very bad state, I could hear everything they talked about, every question they asked my mother about me, even they tried to make contact with me by asking me simple questions, but I could not respond to anything at all, then I suddenly went in a coma, into a very very deep sleep. I passed out on the ambulance bed. There was no more hope for me at all, my mother told me after some time, that they said that it looks like I was not going to make it anyway, because I already lost too much blood.

In my unconscious state God allowed me to go and see how it looked like in hell.

I entered hell and I saw the faces of many souls, old and young burning in flames, I heard them screamed, I saw them vomiting, I saw how the insects and the worms ate their souls . I saw how satan and his demons torched the souls who ended up in hell.

And God allowed me to see it all, He guided and He took me through the valley of the shadow of death. Where darkness lived. As a child back then, Psalm 23 was one of my favorite Psalms, it was always planted and written deep down in my heart and the same Psalm guided me and took me through the valley of the shadow of death, because I stood upon His word that says "I shall fear no evil". in all this times of troubles, even when I was a kid I did not understand what the scripture really meant to me, but God has allowed me to experienced it by myself.

Today I am a living testimony, I am a living proof that His word is a reality and it does remain.

So I faced a near death situation of many others.

And all of a sudden God brought me back to live from my consciousness state, from a bed in hospital where I was laid down with the expectation that I might not make it, but God's hand was upon my life.

When I woke up, I was confused. I looked around and I saw the people around me in devastating situations, I remember, some of the faces I saw in my vision, when God allowed me to enter hell, were exactly from the same faces that night in hospital. I couldn't tell or warn anybody at all , because God did not allowed me to, He closed my mouth, but He shared a secret with me.

My head was rapped up in bandages, I laid on the bed wondering where I was then I heard over the intercom what time and what date it was and what the name of the hospital was, and right there my mind updated itself. "This must be the hospital."

I tried to help myself from the bed, and I acted like I was going to the bathroom, but I started to walk towards the exit door of the hospital. I saw that it was dark outside and the time was around the hour of 2 o' clock in the morning.

I went outside and decided to leave the place immediately, so I started to take off by the road.

Still in a confusing state, I tried to figure out wich way and where to go.

It was Christmas holiday time, and I heard from a far people were singing Christmas carols, so I followed the direction of the voices I heard and it brought me nearer to where I wanted to be.

Then I looked for any lights, and I saw a cross decorated with Christmas lights standing out above the buildings from afar, it was a cross of a church in town, I started to follow the direction to the cross decorated with lights and it brought me to the road side heading back to Wellington, because the hospital was located in Paarl.

Now I knew where I was and I took off by hiking.

Suddenly the day broke through, people started to move on the road, and God in all who He was created everything just right on time.

He allowed an old friend of mine to pass by with his car, on his way to drop off his girlfriend off at work and he stopped at me asking me what happened, I couldn't explained anything to him, but somehow I did remember his face and gave me lift back home.

We first went to his house, where his mother checked on my wounds again, they never stitched it at hospital, they never cleansed it properly at hospital, they just put on a bandage and left me in the hall-way , because they thought I was not going to make it in any way. My friend's mother cleansed the wounds for me, put on some new, fresh and clean bandages, she even gave me taxi fair so that I can go back home.

And I thank God for her kindness and concerned heart.

She made sure that I got safe on the taxi and she told the taxi driver where he had to drop me off and he did.

That morning, was a Monday morning 20 December 1999, for me it was the start of a new life, but an unknown future.

It did not get any better at first, because it was still a long way to go, but it was definitely the first steps into the right direction, to find my way back to myself.

And to find the piece of my heart that was missing.

I came at home and my mother took me to a doctor named Dr. Sarembok in town, she explained everything that happened to me over the period of time from the Thursday 16 December to Monday 20 December 1999 to the doctor.

I was depressed, I was stressed, I was tired, I was exhausted of everything that happened in my life for the past 20 years. The doctor was shocked, he said that it is a miracle that I was actually still alive.

The good news still exist at home, my girlfriend was pregnant and I was about to do the best of something I believed can be the best.

The doctor gave me tablets that I had to drink and he gave me a first aid kid to treat my wounds.

The tablets helped me a lot.

It made me calm and relaxed and it gave me much time to rest.

I was just lying in bed for the rest of the holiday season, wich for me was a good thing, I had time to think about my life, what I was going to do about it.

I still had the job at the factory and we should start later in January 2000.

I became sober during the time and I went to see the doctor often, while I was lying in bed I decided to quit with alcohol, but I still smoked cigarettes.

My head was feeling light and I always had a strange dizzy feeling in my head , but I kept on pushing.

It was one of the toughest things to do for me to quit my bad habit wich was the alcohol because the people around me was still doing their thing, but I took the faith and I did it.

The main reason why I believed that I can "change"was, because of my new born child that was on her way, and I started to talk to God in a way I never done before and I said, "God you know what has brought me to this point in my life, I never knew my biological dad in my life at all, he never showed up to me to be a part of my life, or my mother's life, but today I come to you my Lord, and I may not be where I want to be in life, but I trust your way and I am not going to let my child grow up without her biological father, so you need to help me, so that I can be a present father to my child , please hear my prayer and make it possible for me" Amen.

And that was my prayer to a God, I knew He exist, but I did not know him in person yet, I did not have a close relationship with

Him, but He was there in all the time of my life and I believed it.

Word of encouragement:

John 16: 24 – "Until now you have not asked [the Father] for anything in My name; but now ask and keep on asking and you will receive, so that your joy may be full and complete". No matter where we are in life, there is always the need for a turning point. God is willing and able to do until we stop asking.

the day God called Abraham to leave his family, people and country, was a turning point for Abraham (Genesis 12:1).

In Exodus 3, when God called Moses out of the burning bush to go to Egypt, this was a turning point for the Israelites who for over 400 years had been subjected to slavery and cruel bondage.

Chapter 7

The Ability to move forward:

The new millennium year 2000 has begun, I was doing well, just the fact that my trauma situation became much better and progressive.

Later during the month of January 2000, it was back to work day.

My whole life has changed, I felt like a brand new person at all.

I came at work, nobody knew what I went through during the December holidays ,all they saw was the scars on my forehead and the fact that I didn't drink anymore was for them a completely questionable thing.

They all wanted to figure out what really happened to that old guy they knew for so long.

As a couple of months went by ,it turned out that I began to study the Rastafarians books and I tried to keep myself busy with the religion and lifestyle of the Rastafarians, I even started to have dreadlocks, so I became a Rasta, at least it kept me from the alcohol and other things I was used to and addicted to and all , but I still smoked Marijuana.

I did not overdo the smoking of marijuana at all, but I kept it as low as possible that I could.

My life has changed, I got promoted at the factory I worked at and I became from where I started from as a sander to a quality controller in the department I worked.

I had to check for all components and I had to make sure that it is good enough to go to the spray room to be sprayed.

If the jobs were done spraying then I had to check every item again, and decides if the quality were good enough to go to the the clients.

So I got promoted, the money was a little more and a little extra so I definitely could do better from know. I definitely had a mentor, who I could learn everything about from the spray room and the quality wich was expected, his name was Wayne Jones, I learned a lot from him, I remember when I started working with him , he was the main contact in the spray department and I always respected him, yes there was times when we misunderstood each other, but we could solved our differences easy. Today I can only add the good credit to his life for what he meant in my life.

The only reason that started to matter for me back then, was my girlfriend who was pregnant with a child of mine, and the fact that We were expecting a baby. I had a complete, new outlook on the world I was in, and it gave me a reason to start and live again.

Later the year in August 2000

a beautiful baby was born and we named her Keesha. Such an angel and a gift from God. I remember the morning she was born I went with my girlfriend's family to the hospital to see my new born, so they took me with for the first time, because I never went to their house, I never connected with the family of my girlfriend that close before, we went to hospital and there

God was waiting for me to show me what only He wanted to showed me.

For the first time I could love again, He gave me back a part of myself, a part I was longing for.

My mom was moving out of that small matches box they lived in, into a bigger house wich they started to rent in the area nearby from an old friend we all used to go too.

I didn't go with them, because I wanted to be near to my child and my path with my mother was separated somehow up till today. The relationship between me and mother is still there, it shall always be, but we do not see each other like before, and it started on an early age.

I moved into that small matches box back in the yard of the landlord, where my mother and boyfriend first lived in, for me it was Alright back then, I just needed to be alone and on my own.

I decided to rent the space, I wanted to be alone and on my own and my girlfriend and the little one could come over and we could have some private space.

Three years went by and my little daughter became 3 years old.

During the time of her growth of 3 years, I started to go to their family house , where my girlfriend lived from childhood with her own family.

The family were nice and friendly people at all, they did have their own stuff they dealeth with, but they did not go through what I went through in life at all.

What I sensed about them as a family was that they were bound with love, peace joy and happiness, while I never experienced in my life, they attended the Anglican church.

So I got involved some how with them to the church, and for

the first time I could love again, I felt care, I felt everything I was ever looking for.

My girlfriend came from a well mannered house hold. Their life's was full and complete, they were 6 sisters, Deloris,Lizzy,Roshelle,Pauline,Karen, Felicity and one brother James, a mother and a father.

I respected them in all of my ways I could. Yes I was not perfect at all and I did messed up sometimes, but I trusted that God was in control, not knowing what God was actually up to with my life.

So I did not just go in the house at first when I visited them but I would wait at the door, then she, "my girlfriend" at the time back then would come out to me, and I could see my baby child.

One day my mother in law's brother who was older than her got sick, and because of his age and a stroke he had, he couldn't help himself, my mother in law took him into her house for a while to look after him and she asked me if I don't want to give the old man a bath, because he was not smelling that good at all and I took the honor to do so and I gave him a bath. It went on for a couple of nights, and it was the only time I went inside the house of my in laws.

You know what, and from that first day I entered their house, God came through again for me and He allowed my mother in law to see the good inside of me, for what I was meant to be, a good person and yes she did told me that.

She called me aside and said , "from know on don't come and visit my daughter at the door, but come in and be a real part of your child's life.'

I was overwhelmed, because of just a good deed I've done,

something God expected from me I was just promoted again. I didn't do anything to please someone, but to please God.

So that is who I was supposed to be, a good-hearted person, exactly what my grandma told me just back then before she passed in 1998. She said to me ,You are a good person, one day you shall come far in life.

Like I said she was bedridden and I always helped her with the things she couldn't do.

All the bad things happened in my life was just the lies of the devil who robbed me from my good.

But God was about to restore me again.

In 2003 I made me mind up, went to my girlfriend's father and I asked him for a chance to marry his daughter because I don't want to see my child grow up without me in her life, I added that I want to be part of her life for the rest of my life and I did mean it.

He said, "yes you may, if she want to marry you" and he looked at me with a smile. I didn't wait any longer I told her that I had a talk with her dad and I told him that I want to marry you ,so asked her what do you want to do, and he said "yes."

So I proposed to her, and she said yes.

We had wedding plans ahead of us, I went to my mom and told her the good news, she was so proud of me at all. And my life has changed for the good.

Once I was lost in a world that did not make any sense to me any more , but I found a reason to live and to be happy again.

In the month of November on the 29th day we got married.

The ceremony was very special and simple, but it was awesome, a dream came true for both of us.

We moved into the garage area wich I back then transformed

into a living space on the premises of my in laws.

The garage was build against the servants quarter in the backyard of my in laws. We couldn't move into the servants quarter ,some family members already hired the space ,and they actually waited for a house that has to be given to them, but the agreement from my in laws, was as soon as those family moves out we could move in to the servants quarter and it happened.

After a year and a half we moved into the servants quarter and I had to break through from the garage area to the servant counter and so I made it a bigger living space to lived in.

And the space became a five apartment building.

God was actually good to me, things had really changed in my life.

I started to not going too much to my mother where she stayed , she moved again to go and stay together with her boyfriend at the other side of a new area in Wellington.

It happened that God made a divisions between me and the rest of my own family, because I no longer was visited them at all.

So I became aside, many things and other stuff I just heard from other people about my family. From time to time would pay them a visit.

My brother he also got married and he was staying with his wife all on his own, in the area I stayed with my wife and daughter.

Life surely treated him good, he managed back then to finished his matric, after a year that he couldn't went to school because of the lack of money, and my mother couldn't afford any school fees for him, so he quit school for a year, went out for a work came back paid the the school bill and he finished his matric, got a good job, bought his own house, where he started to live together with his wife and two beautiful and lovely daughters.

So a month before my wedding wich was on 29 November 2003, remember, I was practicing the Rastafarian religion and culture back then, I had to cut my dread locked hair for the big day.

My in laws included my future wife was raised as Anglicans and my daughter was also baptized as Anglican in the name of the Lord and the trinity of Jesus Christ, Father , son and Holy spirit.

Me was also baptized back at childhood at the N.G Sending Church, under the grace of the trinity, Father, son and the Holy Spirit.

So no matter what I had to faced in life, a solid foundation was already laid in my life, I accepted it.

I had to go to the Anglican church for wedding classes . I had to go to the church where I was baptized as a child and asked for my membership certificate, the baptized information and I had to move from the N.G Sending church to the Anglican church in Wellington.

I did all those things for my own good, and the sake of my new family.

I became a member of the Anglican church and I got married with my lovely wife.

We started as family wich God allowed to be, now I had reason to live again.

I became much calm, stopped everything bad that was troubled me, no more marijuana smoking and the only thing on my mind was work, yes I know became a workaholic.

My life was now very relaxed and I could went out on a Saturday with my family to shop's, have a place to go and eat something together, do shopping and all kinds of lovely stuff.

And life was just treating me good,

At work I was promoted again, I became the production point operator in the apartment I worked, so I became the main contact between the floor area and the management in office.

Life began to show me some respect, but all things was not that good as it look like.

We were a very close team and work, but the enemy started to create jealousy and envy between the men on the floor, and I became also a victim.

People would go to the employers office spread false information to the boss and came they would come back to you and talked with you like nothing ever happened, but I always knew everything they did, I just kept the peace.

I always had the conspiracy, the guts , the feeling and I was always blessed to sense the bad energies, I did not know how to used it at all, because you have to know that I was also once bad.

And as good as life was started to treat me, the pain in my heart according the past events in my life was never gone, it still followed me everywhere I went.

I always was reminded of the past and my heart was still troubled with the pain and sorrows.

Word of encouragement:

Isaiah 26:3

If we tend to focus on our troubles, the troubles fill our life lens. But, if we focus on God, He fills our life lens and we stay in His perfect peace. Therefore, when God tells you to move forward, focus on Him.

God has a good plan for your life, and He doesn't want you to be tormented by fear or let it hold you back from your destiny. His will is for you to walk forward, confident in His love, trusting Him to take care of you all along the way.

69

Chapter 8

The realization :
I became fully aware of what God has provided me with, in my heart was the damaged made, in my mind was the battle I still going on, but was somehow connected to His reality.

Sunday mornings, me and my family who was myself, my wife and my daughter as a child would went to the local church in the area where we were members at in church. I had my own talks with God, I really started to have a private relationship with my creator, not knowing where he was about to take me on my life's journey ahead of me, but I started to trusted Him.

Things were just working out for me, of cause it was not all going smooth at all, but I learned from every step he took me through.

I somehow started to win the hearts of many and people and they were starting to look up at me, even in my own the family.

What did I do right? I did not know, but people started to show me love and respect back at home and also at work. God has been good to me, God has been great.

One day while I was sitting all alone by myself in front of the television, my attention was not really towards the television, I tried to figure out what can I do to change my life once and for all, but I did not get any answers at all.

Then something else happened, I had a brother in law, his name was Roger and was married to one of my wife's sisters, and today they are still married and he definitely is still my brother in law, back then he was indeed a man of God.

We all was invited to join his ordination service because he would become a Pastor.

We went to the sermon, it was held on a Sunday morning at "The Breedsaal," wich belonged to the N.G Sending Church. (N.G.Mission church)

So right there in that place God showed me for the first time ever in my life , what he was about to do with my life.

There was a preacher , He was Pastor Gert, the spiritual Father of my brother in law, who spoke the word of God and he spoke about the love of God and what the love of God is all about.

Love was the thing I loosed, love was the thing I was seeking after, Love was the missing piece of my heart to complete the fullness of my heart, I was searching for it, but I couldn't found anything.

He gave his testimony about his life, how he grew up, and what he was and how God saved him from the life he had lived and he also talked about his wife , how he had to look after her, because of the illness she was diagnosed with, and for me by hearing his testimony, something happened inside of me, the feeling inside of me was like God was busy to do an operation on me, and that the messages was definitely ment to be for me.

I went to the bathroom, just to washed my face and my stomach started to pull all together and the feeling was very pain full.

I called out to God while I was in the bathroom and I asked

,God "please help me Lord, I don't know what is happening to me but it hurts, please take this feeling and this pain away from me" and God answered me.

All of a sudden I felt an relief from this thing I experienced.

I was not knowing that it was the past who poisoned the spirit inside of me and God was dealing with it.

I became better, went back into the hall and my brother in law was ordained, He spoke a word of encouragement, he spoke about his life and the vision and mission God has laid upon his heart, and I saw a light in front of the hall coming from both sides of the walls and it covered the lobby of the hall and my eyes could not ignore the light it. I don't know if I was the only one who saw that unusual light that day, but nobody ever spoke about it, so I also kept quiet.

I did not really understand what was happening, but I tried to trust that it had to be something God was revealing to me in the future.

I never talked to anyone about it, but I kept it to myself, today I believe that God wanted me to kept it as secret, because He needed me to trust him.

Time went by and the ghosts of the past was tempting me, things somehow got too much.

My brother in law was the Pastor at his local church located on a farm in Ceres.

Every Sunday and one or two times a week he would go there to the congregation to minister to them.

One day while he was visiting us at home I asked him if it is possible to go with him on the coming Sunday to have a visit at his church and he said "yes you may come.You are more then welcome to join us."

So when the Sunday morning arrived I was all dressed up and ready to go with them and he picked me up with his transport that morning.

As I entered the hall where church was at, I could sense and feel that this is not any usual atmosphere.

In the hall was a presents I never felt before and the people were all happy and everyone carried a smile upon their faces.

The children were so joyful and then a couple of young people including the daughter of my brother in law , who's name is Lynn-lee went to the front of the hall, each of them took a microphone , young men went on the stage in front of the hall and they started to sing songs that really touched my inner human being.

They started with joyful dancing songs, then I learned that they called it praise. I didn't know what was praise at all.

After a while the atmosphere in the room had a shift and they started to sing slower songs, and now all of a sudden this songs was sad and it made people cried, but did not understand what's happening.

For a moment this songs brought me to a place where I could feel very emotional and God allowed me to take a look into my past life and where I found myself on this morning.

Then I come to my sense that this have to be worshiping God on a higher level.

My brother in law went to the front and he then took the microphone and he opened up his mouth.

I felt that another presents was hitting the hall and the presents of something I never imagine it could really exist hit the atmosphere in the hall. It was the presents of the living God, people started to fell on the ground, some felt from their chairs and all of a sudden it happened that I was moved and I found myself in the front of the hall with my hands in the air in the form of surrendering.

So the band dropped and my brother in law told the congregation who I was, and then he asked me what am I doing here in the front of the church.

I answered him with tears who rolled over my cheeks, I said, "Pastor I need to change my life for good, but I don't know how, everything is just too much for me."

My brother in law asked me,

"Is it possible for you to repent your sins and give Jesus a fair chance in your life."

I said "yes Pastor, I want to repent and start my life over again."

So this was the day I gave my heart to Jesus, not knowing what it is about to happen next, but I started to put my trust in something I knew could exist and could make me feel better.

I repented, received Jesus as my personal saviour and I was born again on 3 May 2009.

It was just the beginning of another chapter in my life, not knowing what lies ahead of me, but somehow God has restored me from the pain, the anger, the blame and the sins I carried.

The foundation was laid down long ago when I was just a small little boy.

And over the years the foundation was just standing still, no bricks was laid upon the foundation, but on this, the day I became born again it was the day the first bricks were laid and I started to build what God had in mind for me. I took the faith that I had inside of me and I put it to action, and I believed in something greater that I was.

Things was not going all smooth and sound but it definitely

went better.

Word of encouragement:

Hebrews 11:1-3 Faith is the realization of what is hoped for and evidence of things not seen. Because of it the ancients were well attested. By faith we understand that the universe was ordered by the word of God, so that what is visible came into being through the invisible.

It is the dawning of Truth in the consciousness. When re-alization takes place, one abides in the light of the mind of God. It is the inner conviction that prayer has been answered, although there is as yet no outer manifestation. The supreme realization is unity with God-Mind, complete oneness with the Christ consciousness

Chapter 9

The recognizen:

I became part of this new family of mine, "A living Sacrifice Family church," we were located in Ceres on a farm.

Every Sunday mornings and also during the week we traveled all the way to Ceres to serve God's people.

It took a lot of sacrifices and confidence to do what we did back then, but with the help of God everything became easier and it and possible. I always believed that everything we had put in will someday pay off.

At work people looked at me with new eyes, I started to live my life as a child of God and they had much respect for me.

At home things were just blessed.

Good things started to happen in my household and the peace of the Lord was ever present.

We as a church used to organized family gatherings and we used to take our families out on a Sunday if it was possible and than all of us would have lunch together.

My mother in law, aunt Dottie as most people knew her, her actual name was Dorothy, she and her good old friend we called aunt Gitsy they always joined us and they were so glad to always be around us.

They just enjoyed what we were busy with.

Yes we all was so bounded in God's love together as one.

My life changed radical.

I was baptized again as an adult and my believe in the Lord my saviour gave me the assurance that, the trust and the hope in believing that the old me does not exist anymore, because of the faith I took that the old person who was has died with Christ. All things became new for me.

We used to go out and preached the gospel of Christ in places , then we gave our testimonies to those who needed it and we reach out to many people as far as Calvinia and Midddlepost.

As the the time went by I was promoted at church, from a normal brother to the deacon of the Church. I was ordained as deacon on 28 February 2010.

Things started to move for me into another direction, because now I saw that God really had a purpose for my life.

I remember we had an Evangelistic tent service in Tullbagh, Western Cape back then, on a Easter weekend and then we slept out in the tent away from home.

Pastor told me that we would finish off our weekend services with an evangelistic service on the coming Sunday evening and I have to prepare myself because God has laid it upon his heart that I had to minister the word.

So my other brother in Christ , who's name was Ashley, who was also a deacon together with me would preach a preface and I will be preach the Main word of the evening. It was on an Easter weekend, I remember.

That night God showed up again for me , to show me I was capable of in and through Him.

When the time arrived and I had to go forward, I felt God putting his arms around me as I walked to the front, I took the microphone open my mouth and I started to sing "Majesty we worship you Majesty" and the presents of God immediately filled the tent and his glory came down from heaven and without saying anything people started to fall over each other , some was crying and screaming and God showed me what He was capable to do through me if I would allow him to do so.

So I started to preach only around one verse about the man upon the cross and God hitted again, people was saved, people was delivered people had an encounter with their creator in a super natural encounter.

I was just me, coming out of a disaster of life and a mess in life, but all that things I went through was to create and call the Anointing wich he placed upon my life to existence.

After that event we reached out to many different places who was in different situations and circumstances.

We held house prayer times at people's houses and God showed us great things and miracles.

Then I got promoted again and was ordained as the elder of the church.

I was eventually stepping up the leader.

My household was getting in good shape, everything started to work out for me, but the enemy, wich we still call the devil in todays life, who is satan was never pleased and satisfied with what God was busy doing in my life.

At work I became the main spray painter at the factory and I started to spray the final coats of the sprayed furniture that needs to be sprayed, and with the knowledge I had about the quality that needs to be delivered I did great.

In the mornings before we started to take the task for the day to hand, I called upon a prayer meeting with the help of another brother who used to be a friend of mine back then and he also managed to become a Pastor. Densil was his name.

He was the one ,who once offered a place for me and mother and brother to stayed at his family's home back then.

We worked together and we took the privilege to held every morning a prayer meeting before we started the day and its work and the staff on the floor joined us.

We all became close to each other at the factory wich were Prowell woodworkers, back then.

We were like brothers of the same mother, we could talk cry and laugh together. Most of times were spent at the factory.

As the time went by, me was the elder of the church. My pastor who became my spiritual Father started to work out to different kinds of places around the region, so there was no more way to go to Ceres to see to the need of the congregation in Ceres, so they had to go on all by themselves, when pastor came back from where he was we then took the opportunity and we would go and see how things were doing in Ceres.

But things started to go wrong somehow, The he decided that the team from Wellington who usually traveled to Ceres, had to find a place to worship God in Wellington.

We found a space at Pauw Gedenk Primary school and we had our services there.

Slowly but surely satan was planning to sink the boat, he was never satisfied with my life at all, and what God was busy doing.

Something else happened to me. I started to feel as my stomach was bloated and the feeling don't want to go away at all.

So I didn't know what was really happening, I went to the doctor and they told me it was just air on my stomach it will go away soon. The doctor gave me medicine that I had to use and I did.

So I took the words of the doctor and made it my own but nothing went away.

So someone gave me some advice about what I maybe could try to do.

Never had I imagined that it was satan planning to trap me again and he planned it well.

So he used a friend of mine at work to try to mislead me from the way I was on.

God has saved me already, God has healed me already, but what satan knew was I was healed, but the wounds in my mind and in my heart was still raw.

So he took the advantage to attack and strike again before the wound could heal completely.

Gods plan, was to take me somewhere, satans plan was to keep me from where God was taking me.

It started all with an bloated stomach.

Spiritual I was on another level, but you know what, my flesh was still weak and he exactly knew that, so he need to strike at the weak point, my heart was on the right way but I still needed to get rid of things I used to do.

The small things that I didn't know was that big of an issue, he started to use it against me.

Word of encouragement:

Proverb 3 : 5

"Trust in the LORD with all your heart and lean not on your own understanding"

The verse instructs us to put all our trust in the Lord and not our own knowledge. The verse tells us not to be reliant on our strength and knowledge, but to trust in the Lord.

Isaiah:12-18

Once we recognize God as the source of our life, our knowledge and our wisdom, it gives us a new perspective on our work.

He is the one who has gone before us and shown us what lies beyond our suffering and He's the one who will "strengthen us with power through his Spirit in our inner being" (Ephesians 3:16), is constantly "at work within us" (Ephesians 3:20) and will perfect us as we cling to Him in the midst of our trials...

Chapter 10

The acception:

I accepted God the Father though Jesus Christ to came into my heart.

By His spirit he led me from the wilderness wich I found myself in, to a place He called the desert , so their must be a paradise. In the next edition of my book The missing piece I will tell you about the dessert I went through, and the promise of the paradise He has in mind for me.

I was overwhelmed by His love, His grace and His mercy upon my life, then, the piece of my heart that was missing and the emptiness I felt was starting to dissapear and the hole was filled up with light again. The feeling I experienced was speechless, because for once an for all I could feel comfortable by having Him, God the Father in my life, He was like the missing part I was searhing for all my life, because my relationship with him was open to Him like I could talked to Him like a son could talk to his father. He filled the hole I had in my heart as a father figure, I was not scared anymore because He provided me of the protection I needed, I was not violent anymore because my relationship with Him gave me the peace I was looking for, but satan was not satisfied with it at all.

In the next book I will write to you about how satan struck again, how he targeted me, what he did towards my life, what I went through, where I ended up several on several times.

I will tell you in the next book how I was tempted again and how I stood face to face with the devil himself.

I will write how he wanted to steal the joy from my life and how he planned to vanished me from the face of the earth.

I will tell you how he wanted to destroy my life completely, how he wanted to destroy my marriage and how he wanted to brought the people God placed in my life for his glory turn against me. But God took the good that He placed inside of me and gave me the authority to use against the plan of satan.

I will tell you in the next addition of my book how I ended up in several near dead situations, how God had one on one encounters with me and how God called me out for His purpose and how God called me to minister. Today I am pleased in Christ to say I am loaded with His anointing to cancel the works of evil.

God always had the bigger picture in mind.

I am glad I accepted Him, I am ministering the word of God on several occasions, I encourages people around the world on a platform like Facebook and I have several things going on.

And as I believe that there is a great future ahead, I will tell you in the next book, about how God opened my spiritual eyes and ears and how I communicate with the angels God encountered me with.

God has really been good to me.

I want to tell you today, as you are reading this book of mine.

Never, ever give up on yourself. Never give up on your dreams and your hopes.

Never give up on your children or their children.

Never give up on your mother or your father. Never give up

on anything.

If you never had a mother or a father in your life that you can call a parent, do not think that life has ended for you, it is actually the start of something greater in your life, do not blame anyone but consult God. Every coming to us on our life path is a learning process and God want us to figure it out in Him. He does have all the answers according our lives, that we can be sure of.

I have found my completeness and the missing part in my life at the cross, at the cross he took everything that I faced and even what I still had to face, He took it come upon Him,

and just that part, made my heart whole again, the light came through and now I need to protect the cross that made my life full and complete, I have to learn how to use the cross to be completely healed, the dessert experience will tell you how it all went, maybe I am not fully where I want to be in life, but I am exactly where I must be and I have the assurance that all things will work out for those who believe.

To be continued....

Word of encouragement:

Romans 15:7,

"Therefore, accept one another, just as Christ also accepted us to the glory of God." Romans 10:13, For "everyone who calls on the name of the Lord will be saved." Romans 15:7, "Therefore, accept one another, just as Christ also accepted us to the glory of God."

Romans 14:1-2

1 Accept the one whose faith is weak, without quarreling over

disputable matters.

Romans 3:23 For all have sinned and fall short of the glory of God. For everyone has sinned; we all fall short of God's glorious standard. For all have sinned and fall short of the glory of God. For all have sinned, and come short of the glory of God.

Romans 8:28

28 And we know that God causes everything to work together for the good of those who love God and are called according to his purpose for them. 28 That's why we can be so sure that every detail in our lives of love for God is worked into something good.

God bless every Reader of this book and may you be healed, restored and delivered from whatever troubled your mind and heart, by the words of this book and the Grace of God, the Father, The Son and the Holy Spirit

In the mighty name of Jesus Christ.

Amen.

My message of Faith, hope and love to you.

Your life was set by God, and He called you for a very great and powerful and purpose in in life, towards your destiny.

You were called to be a living Sacrifice, but also a living proof of His work, so that His name can be glorified, to be a testimony in life to safe another soul from the reality of hell.

There is for every one out there a bright future, but our choices and our decisions is the drive behind the directions to our destiny in the future.

So do not give up on your parent, don't give up on your child, don't give up on a friend or a family member, don't give up on your future and most importantly, never give up on God.

You don't have to be a part of the world around you to fit in, You don't have to do sex, drugs and alcohol, You don't have to be a thief or a murderer or a prostitute or any bad person. God loves you and He wants you to bring the best of His goodness wich He placed inside of you, out of yourself.

He has locked up the best of yourself inside of you, it is for you to bring it to existence.

You are filled with many talents and gifts, but it can only get out of you when you allow Him to unlock it for you.

This is my personal word of encouragement to you today.

All things are possible for God, if you allow Him to.

You can do it.

You can win it.

Because you have the winner on your side.

Proverbs 3:5-6 Trust in the Lord with all of your heart and do not lean on your own understanding. In all your ways acknowledge Him, and He will make your paths straight.

Shane Marquin van Rooyen